# The Great Wizard Of The Wall

TED MORRISON

To order additional copies of this book, contact:
Xlibris
844-714-8691
www.Xlibris.com
Orders@Xlibris.com

ISBN: 978-1-6698-2382-7 (sc)
ISBN: 978-1-6698-2383-4 (hc)
ISBN: 978-1-6698-2381-0 (e)

Library of Congress Control Number: 2023901221

Print information available on the last page

Rev. date: 02/10/2023

# The Great Wizard Of The Wall

The
Great Wizard
Of the Wall

Once upon a time, in a beautiful place called "Freedom Land" live the Great Wizard of the wall, Freedom Land was a very beautiful place where people from all over the world would come and visit, some would even stay.

Freedom Land was such a wonderful place, full of fun and amusement.

People of all races, religions, and cultures would travel thousands of miles to experience all of the things that Freedom Land had to offer.

Freedom Land was a place where the world's best doctors, lawyers, scientists, builders, cooks, dancers, singers and athletes resided, "It was a paradise on earth."

Freedom Land functioned under a merit system, if you had a special gift, skill or talent to offer, Freedom Land was the place for you.

The Wizard of the wall was assigned the task of evaluation and approval of all who wished to enter Freedom Land.

It was here at the port of entry where all visitors to Freedom Land would come, introduce themselves, their gifts, skills and talents.

One day there came a knock at the door, (Knock, Knock, Knock) "Who's there yelled the Wizard?" It is I, Media Man Mr. Wizard.

"How can I help you," asked the Wizard? I'm here to offer Freedom Land my expertise in communications programming, said Media Man.

I assure you that it will be very helpful and beneficial to Freedom Land Mr. Wizard.

"What kind of programming do you offer to Freedom Land," asked the Wizard?

"I'm glad you asked," said Media Man.

Why I offer a variety of entertainment programs such as basketball, baseball, football, soccer, hockey and a host of other athletic programs.

In addition to that said Media Man, I offer programming of the Arts, Dance Music and Science.

"What programs do you offer in the field of education," asked the Wizard? "I'm glad you asked," said Media Man.

I offer all sorts of tutorial programming such as reading, spelling, math, social studies and science. "Well," said the Wizard, I must say that I'm impressed.

I will allow you entry into Freedom Land.

Once he was allowed entry into Freedom Land, Media Man immediately began observing the ways and actions of the people of Freedom Land.

Media Man began to study their religions, culture, eating and social habits.

Once all of this information was obtained, Media Man went and had an office and a communication tower built in the very center of Freedom Land.

Once the building of his office and tower was complete, Media Man asked the approval of the Wizard to place communication devices into the homes of the residences of Freedom Land.

"Why is all of this necessary" asked the Wizard?

Media Man explained that it would make it easier to deliver his programming on a broader scale.

The Wizard said "Okay Media Man," you have my permission.

Media Man immediately began installing his communication devices into all of the homes of the residence of Freedom Land.

Once all of the devices were installed, Media Man returned to his tower of programming, where he began to send out frequencies to all of the homes of the residence of Freedom Land.

With these frequencies, Media Man was now able to start introducing his new programming methods to all of the residence of Freedom Land.

All of the residents of Freedom Land began to celebrate and praise their new found friend Media Man for enriching their lives through these new communication devices.

On every station and every channel, tutorial programs would run night and day all year round.

Through these new communication devices the residents of Freedom Land began to learn new methods of how to cook, dance, build, entertain and educate themselves.

The lives of the residence of Freedom Land appeared to be enriched by Media Man's new programming devices.

Over a period of time the Wizard started to notice a change in the health and behaviors of the residence of Freedom Land.

The new entertainment and tutorial programming began to have a chronic and sometimes permanent effect on the residence of Freedom Land.

The residence had began to spend more time indoors than out.

They would spend hours upon hours on couches, across beds watching and listening to the newly installed communication devices.

This appeared to have a profound effect on their health.

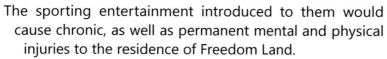

The sporting entertainment introduced to them would cause chronic, as well as permanent mental and physical injuries to the residence of Freedom Land.

The tutorial programming which was once simple, became very difficult and too complex to comprehend.

The ways in which the newly built homes in which the residence of Freedom Land were living in, were built of an inferior material recommended through the new building programs introduced by Media Man's new devices.

The buildings very fragile and vulnerable to the natural elements of nature.

The newly introduced music, movies and fashion, tore away at the very fabric of the culture of the residence of Freedom Land.

The crime in Freedom Land began to escalate to unprecedented levels.

Freedom Land was no longer a place where the world's people wanted to visit, or to stay, this angered the Wizard very much.

The Wizard went to see Media Man about what was going on with the newly installed programming devices and the adverse effect it was having on the residence of the Freedom Land.

The Wizard explained how the new programming was causing the residence to lie, cheat, sreal, use drugs and commit violent acts upon one another.

Media Man told the Wizard that he was not aware of this and that he would review the programming and get back to him right away.

The Wizard was very suspicious of Media Man, finding his explanation unacceptable.

Feeling that something just wasn't right with Media Man, the Wizard decided that he would hang around awhile and observe the goings on there at Media Man's Office.

Later on the day, the Wizard observed Media Man leaving his office and walk down a very dark hallway where he then entered a room where he met a group of individuals whose identities could not be revealed.

Media Man began to tell this group of people that the Wizard had grown suspicious of them and their programs and wanted to know what was going on.

The Wizard grew even more upset at what he saw and heard from Media Man.

Media Man began to tell this group of people that the Wizard had grown suspicious them and their programs and wanted to know what was going on.

The Wizard could not believe that the man he had entrusted the lives of the residence of Freedom Land to, had deceived him and had designed a plan to harm them.

The Wizard immediately left Media Man's office building and summoned his security forces to put a stop to this evil plan of Media Man and his accomplices.

The Wizard and his security officers devised a plan to stop Media Man and his evil accomplices.

The first thing the Wizard decided to do was to inform all of the residence of Freedom Land of Media Man's true intentions.

The Wizard had all of the residents turn in all of the communication devices Media Man had installed in their homes.

The Wizard also had all of the music, movies, books and videos sold to the residents of Freedom Land collected and destroyed.

The Wizard then had his security forces storm the office building of Media Man and placed him and his evil accomplices under arrest.

The Wizard then had his security forces tear down Media Man's communication tower, never to be re-opened again.

The next day Media Man and all of his accomplices were rounded up and escorted back to the port of entry of Freedom Land, where they were expelled, never to return again.

Media Man began to beg for another chance, promising to introduce more positive programs.

The Wizard gently placed his hand on Media Man's shoulder, walked him back to the port of entry, gently turned Media Man around and Kicked him right over the wall.

Early the next day, as the sun began to rise, there was a calm over the air of Freedom Land, something the residents hadn't experienced in years.

They knew that they had been badly deceived by Media Man and vowed to rebuild and overcome the evil plans Media Man and his accomplices had devised to destroy their beloved Freedom Land.

The residents all gathered, joined hands and began to pray for the healing of their beloved Freedom Land.

They began to sing songs of love, joy, peace and hope for a brighter tomorrow for their beloved Freedom Land.

This here touched his heart and pleased the Wizard so much that a tear of joy dropped from his eye.

Today Freedom Land is once again a paradise where people from all over the world come to enjoy peace, freedom, joy and happiness.

The End..

Printed in the United States
by Baker & Taylor Publisher Services